TRANSLATED BY

DAVID WALSER

VIKING

Jan Pieńkowski
The Fairy Tales

FOR

Abigail and Tom ⋆ Rose and Louis
Madeleine and Hattie
Eve

VIKING
Published by Penguin Group
Penguin Young Readers Group, 345 Hudson Street, New York, New York 10014, U.S.A.
Penguin Group (Canada), 90 Eglinton Avenue East, Suite 700, Toronto, Ontario, Canada M4P 2Y3
(a division of Pearson Penguin Canada Inc.)
Penguin Books Ltd, 80 Strand, London WC2R 0RL, England
Penguin Ireland, 25 St Stephen's Green, Dublin 2, Ireland (a division of Penguin Books Ltd)
Penguin Group (Australia), 250 Camberwell Road, Camberwell, Victoria 3124, Australia
(a division of Pearson Australia Group Pty Ltd)
Penguin Books India Pvt Ltd, 11 Community Centre, Panchsheel Park, New Delhi – 110 017, India
Penguin Group (NZ), Cnr Airborne and Rosedale Roads, Albany, Auckland 1310, New Zealand
(a division of Pearson New Zealand Ltd)
Penguin Books (South Africa) (Pty) Ltd, 24 Sturdee Avenue, Rosebank, Johannesburg 2196, South Africa

Penguin Books Ltd, Registered Offices: 80 Strand, London WC2R 0RL, England

"Sleeping Beauty," "Snow White," "Hansel and Gretel," and "Cinderella"
first published by William Heinemann Ltd and Gallery Five Ltd 1977
Originally published in this form in the U.K. in 2005 by Puffin Books
This edition published in the U.S.A. in 2006 by Viking, a division of Penguin Young Readers Group

1   3   5   7   9   10   8   6   4   2

Text copyright © David Walser, 1977, 2005
Illustrations copyright © Jan Pienkowski, 1977, 2005
All rights reserved

ISBN: 0-670-06189-1

Hand lettering by Jane Walmsley
Manufactured in China

The Storytellers

CHARLES PERRAULT AND THE BROTHERS GRIMM are two of the most famous names in the world of fairy tale. Between them they have gathered hundreds of traditional folk tales from all across Europe, writing them down where previously the stories had been passed to each new generation by word of mouth. It is probably thanks to their actions that we still enjoy the wonder and enchantment of *Snow White*, delight in the danger and romance of *Sleeping Beauty* and share in the strength and courage of *Hansel and Gretel*.

Perrault's earliest collection, *Tales from Times Past, With Morals*, first appeared in France in 1697. It was a small volume of eight stories that were originally written for the court of Versailles. The entire court was taken with the drama and wit of Perrault's magical tales and his popularity as a storyteller soon spread across France and into Europe. This collection later became known as *Tales from Mother Goose*, a title more familiar to us today.

No one really knows exactly where Perrault collected his stories, but we do know that the Brothers Grimm gathered over 200 stories from within their native Germany. Jacob and Wilhelm shared a passion for folklore and they searched constantly for new stories to add to their growing collection.

They travelled far and wide, visiting many a small village and farmhouse where women sat and spun yarn by the fireside, recounting traditional stories. They welcomed friends, neighbours and those with a gift for storytelling into their home. They wanted to capture the unique feel of each fairy tale and wrote them down with the greatest of care. Like Charles Perrault, they succeeded in capturing a fantastical world of danger, romance and excitement, creating a wave of interest in the great oral tradition of Europe and inspiring a whole new generation of storytelling.

Even though the fairy tales of Charles Perrault appeared over 100 years before the Brothers Grimm published their *German Popular Stories*, differing versions of some of the same classic tales can be found in both volumes. In this collection we have used Perrault's gentler, more romantic version of *Cinderella*, rather than the gruesome tale retold by the Brothers Grimm, which ended with the two stepsisters having their eyes pecked out by birds! In later years, Wilhelm Grimm softened their retellings to suit a new and younger audience. He removed the more frightening details, but true to the original intentions of the Brothers Grimm, the stories in this collection – *Sleeping Beauty*, *Hansel and Gretel* and *Snow White* – appear in their earlier versions with all the grizzly details left in.

CHARLES PERRAULT *1628–1703*
JACOB LUDWIG CARL GRIMM *1785–1863*
& WILHELM CARL GRIMM *1786–1859*

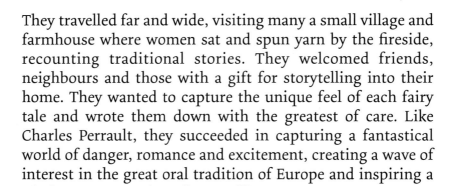

vii

Until the age of eight I lived in the country surrounded by woods, first in Poland, then in Austria, then Bavaria. The forest was my playground, my jungle and the stuff of nightmares. The dappled light, dense shade and the wind in the tall trees were a secret world, inhabited by all kinds of strange and wonderful creatures.

My silhouettes may well have been inspired by the forest. Looking at a sunny clearing out of the dark woodland simplifies reality into black and white. The profile becomes everything. Perhaps this explains the prevalence of the silhouette as a traditional art form in the heart of Europe, from the Black Forest to South Poland.

From earliest childhood, I remember sitting around a table cutting out Christmas decorations from drab wartime paper. Our kitchen had cut-out paper curtains that were changed at Whitsun every year by a local paper cutter; I watched with fascination as she folded the paper and cut it with enormous shears before unfolding it to reveal birds and flowers on a perfect lattice, ready to be pinned up in the window.

In Warsaw, during the rising in 1944, we had all gone into the shelter. Someone contrived to entertain the children by cutting out animals from paper with a pair of nail scissors. My mother and I hated the shelter, and we never went there again, but I loved the cut-out creatures.

Early in my career, I was offered a manuscript to illustrate and was asked to do a sample piece. I got the picture done just in time, but the faces were not right. At the last second I had an inspiration and filled them in with black Indian ink. Then I drove to the publisher with the wet picture, hoping it would dry in time. It did and I got the job!

Jan Pieńkowski

BOTH MY PARENTS WERE BORN OF FRENCH MOTHERS, and my father's father, who emigrated to England, was German-speaking Swiss, so I grew up in a household in which both German and French were commonplace.

After the Second World War, my father was with the occupying forces in Germany. I was at boarding school in England, but went out to Germany for the holidays. On the way, I would stop off in France to visit my relations and feast myself on *Tintin* and *Asterix*. This is also when I made my first acquaintance with the stories of Charles Perrault.

I later became great friends with a pair of German twins from Schramberg, in the Black Forest. I often went to stay with their family and, every weekend, their father, Helmut, would drag us out on walks through the forest, sometimes lasting all day. Once we emerged into a clearing where there was a small hamlet. One of the farmhouses served delicious sausages, crusty bread and freshly brewed beer, all of the farmer's own making. We sat in a huge room that had a wooden floor, a wooden ceiling an inch or two above my head and proper double windows on three sides. We were served by a bent old woman who reminded me exactly of the witch in *Hansel and Gretel*. I wondered if I would end up in the next batch of sausages and, if so, would I taste as good!

Years later, another German friend gave me a copy of the original edition of *Grimm's Fairy Tales* and encouraged me to persevere with the dialects in which many of the stories are written. In this collection I have tried to preserve the peculiar qualities of the original phrasing of both the Brothers Grimm and Charles Perrault, to reflect the strange, dark and magical atmosphere of the original retellings.

David Walser

Sleeping Beauty

Told by

THE BROTHERS GRIMM

nce upon a time there lived a king and queen who said to one another every day: "If only we were blessed with a child," but sadly they were not.

Then, one day, while the queen was taking her bath, a frog climbed out of the water on to the rim of the bath and said to her: "Your wish will be granted.

Before one year is passed, you will give birth to a daughter."

What the frog foretold came to pass.

2

The queen bore a daughter who was so beautiful that the king was beside himself with joy and decided to hold a splendid banquet. He invited his relatives, his friends and also the Wise Women.

He hoped they would be well disposed towards the child. In his kingdom there were thirteen Wise Women, but because he only had twelve golden plates from which they must eat, the king invited all of the Wise Women except one, who had to stay at home.

The banquet took place with great ceremony, and when it was over the Wise Women presented the child with their magic gifts.

4

One gave virtue, another beauty,
a third riches,

and so on
until the child
had everything that one
could wish for in the whole world.
But when the eleventh Wise Woman
had made her gift, the thirteenth
Wise Woman suddenly swept
into the hall.

She was set on revenge for not having been invited. Without so much as a greeting or a glance at anyone, she shouted out: "The daughter of the king will prick her finger on a spindle in her fifteenth year, and she will die."

With that, she turned on her heel and left the banquet hall.

Everyone was struck dumb with shock, when up stepped the twelfth Wise Woman, who had not yet made her gift.

While she could not wipe out the wicked gift, she could make it less severe, and so she said: "The princess will not die but sink into a sleep that will last a hundred years."

The king,
who would
gladly
have
saved his
child from
this great
misfortune,
commanded
that all the
spindles in
the kingdom
be burnt.

In the meantime, the gifts of the Wise Women were fulfilled, and the girl grew up so beautiful and virtuous and friendly and wise that all who saw her loved her.

Now it happened that on the very day she turned fifteen, she found herself alone in the castle, for the king and queen were away. The girl explored every room, both large and small, every nook and every cranny she could find, until at last she came to an old tower.

She climbed the flight
of narrow winding stairs
until she came to a little
doorway. In the lock
there was a rusty key.
When she turned it,
the door sprang open.

There in a tiny room sat an old woman with a spindle, busily spinning flax.

"Good day to you, little old mother," said the king's daughter. "What are you doing there?"

"I am spinning," said the old woman, with a nod of her head.

"What is that, that jumps about so fast?" asked the girl, and, as she asked, she took hold of the spindle and tried to work it for herself. But hardly had she moved it before the curse upon her was fulfilled. She pricked her finger and in the same instant she sank down upon a bed and fell into a deep sleep.

And this sleep spread throughout the castle to all the people of the court and

to the king and queen as
they came home and entered
the hall.

One and all fell into a deep sleep:

the horses in the stalls,
the hounds in the courtyard,

the doves on the rooftops, the flies
on the wall. Even the fire that flickered
in the hearth stilled itself and slept.
The roast stopped spitting, and the
cook who was pulling the kitchen boy's
hair, because of some slip he had
made, let him go and fell asleep.

The wind too was stilled,
and not a leaf stirred on the trees.

Around the castle
a hedge of thorns
began to grow apace,
and every year
it grew higher and higher until it
surrounded the whole castle, and grew
so tall that not a thing could be seen
— not even the flags on the rooftops.

The story of the Sleeping Beauty, for so she was called, spread throughout the land, so that from time to time young princes came there and tried to force their way through the thorn hedge and into the castle.

I t was not possible, for the thorns held them fast as if with hands so that the young men were trapped, unable to free themselves, and they all died a wretched death.

After many a long year, a young prince came to those parts. He heard an old man tell how a great castle stood behind the thorn hedge, and that in the castle there was a beautiful princess called the Sleeping Beauty, who had to sleep for one hundred years, and how the king and queen and all the people of the court slept too.

The old man had also heard, from his grandfather, how many young princes had come to that place

and tried to force their way through the thorn hedge, and how they were trapped and held there until they died a wretched death.

The young man said: "I am not afraid. I shall go to the castle and I shall see the Sleeping Beauty."

The good old man tried to dissuade him, but to no avail. The young man would not listen.

Just at this time, the hundred years were passed and the day had come when the Sleeping Beauty should awake. When the young prince reached the hedge, the thorns burst into flower, untangled themselves before his eyes and let him pass unharmed, closing again behind him.

In the castle yard, he saw the
horses and the brindled hounds lying
there asleep. On the rooftops sat
the doves with their heads tucked
under their wings. When he went into
the castle, he saw the flies asleep
on the wall; he saw the cook with his
hand still held high, as if about to strike
the kitchen boy, and the kitchen maid
sitting in front of a black hen she was

about to pluck. He went into the hall
where the whole court lay sleeping,
and there beside the throne lay the
king and queen.

He went on again. All was so
still you could hear yourself breathe.
At last he came to the tower and
opened the door to the little room,
where he found the princess asleep
on the bed.

There she lay,
so beautiful that
he could not drag
his eyes from her.

Then he stooped down
and gave her a kiss,

and, as if stirred by the kiss,
the Sleeping Beauty awoke

and looked at the young prince
with friendly eyes.

Together they
went down to the hall, and
the king and queen awoke and all
the courtiers too, and looked at each
other with wonder.

The horses in the courtyard stood up and shook themselves; the hounds sprang up and wagged their tails; the doves on the rooftops pulled out their heads from beneath their wings, gazed about them and flew down into the meadows;

the flies on the walls began to
crawl about again; the fire in
the kitchen grate flared and heated
the pot; the roast began to spit;

the cook slapped the kitchen
boy across the ear so that he cried
out; and the maid finished plucking
the hen.

Soon afterwards, the wedding of the young prince and the Sleeping Beauty was held with great pomp and ceremony, and the two of them lived happily to the end of their days.

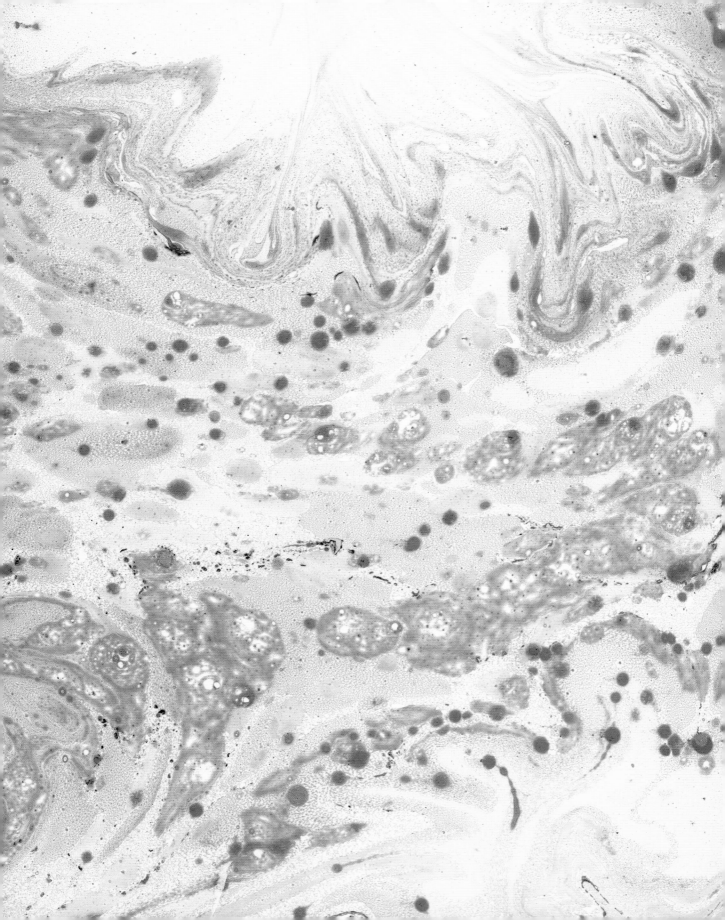

Snow White

now

hite

Told by

THE BROTHERS GRIMM

It was deep midwinter, and snowflakes were falling like feathers from the sky. A queen sat sewing at her window, which had a fine black ebony frame. As she gazed out at the white landscape, she pricked her finger with the needle and three drops of blood fell on the snow.

"If only I had a child as white as snow, as red as blood and as black as ebony," she thought.

Not long after, her wish was granted, for a daughter was born to her. The child's skin was as white as snow, her lips and cheeks as red as blood and her hair as black as ebony, so she was called Snow White. But as she was born, the queen died.

After a year, the king married again.
His new wife was a beautiful woman,
though so proud and overbearing
that she could not endure any rival
to her beauty.

The new queen had a magic mirror, and when she stood before it gazing at her own reflection she would ask:

"Mirror, Mirror, on the wall,
Who is the fairest one of all?"

It always replied:

"You, my Lady Queen,
are the fairest one of all."

Then she was happy, for she knew the mirror always spoke the truth.

But Snow White was growing prettier and prettier every day. When she was seven years old she was as beautiful as a bright day and fairer even than the queen herself. One day, when the queen asked her mirror the question, it replied:

"Though you, my Queen,
are fair, 'tis true,
Snow White is fairer far than you."

The queen flew into a dreadful rage and turned green and yellow with jealousy. From this hour forth, she hated the girl, and envy and malice grew like weeds in her heart so that she had no more peace, day or night.

One day she called a huntsman to her and said: "Take the child out into the forest; I never want to see her face again. You must kill her and bring me back her lungs and liver as proof she is dead."

The huntsman did as he was told and led Snow White into the forest, but as he was drawing his hunting knife to slay her, she cried out:

"Good huntsman, spare my life and I will run into the wild forest and never go home again."

She looked so pretty that the huntsman had pity on her, and said: "Well, run away, you poor child."

But he said to himself: "The wild beasts will soon eat her up," and his heart felt lighter, because he hadn't had to kill her himself.

As he turned away, a young boar came running past, so he shot it and brought its lungs and liver home to the queen as a proof that Snow White was really dead. The cook was told to stew them in salt and the wicked woman ate them up, thinking she had eaten Snow White's lungs and liver.

Now the poor child found herself alone in the forest, and she felt so frightened she didn't know which way to turn. She began to run over the sharp stones and through bramble bushes; the wild beasts ran close by her, but they did her no harm.

Snow White ran as far as her legs would carry her and, as evening approached, she saw a little house and went inside to rest.

Everything was very small in the little house, but cleaner and neater than anything you can imagine. In the middle of the room, there stood a little table with a white tablecloth and seven little plates, each with its fork, spoon, knife and cup. Side by side against the wall, there were seven little beds, covered with shining white counterpanes.

Snow White felt so hungry and thirsty that she ate a bit of bread and some porridge from each plate and drank a drop of wine out of each cup, for she didn't want to leave anyone without food or drink. Then, feeling tired, she lay down on one of the beds, but it wasn't comfortable. She tried all the others in turn; one was too long and another too short, until she tried the seventh, which was just right. So she lay down upon it, said her prayers and fell asleep.

When it was quite dark, the masters of the little house returned. They were seven dwarfs who worked high up in the mountains.

They lit their seven little lamps and saw
that someone had been there, for the
room was not as they had left it.

The first said: "Who's been sitting on
my chair?"

The second said: "Who's been eating
out of my plate?"

The third said: "Who's been eating
my bread?"

The fourth said: "Who's been tasting
my porridge?"

The fifth said: "Who's been using my fork?"

The sixth said: "Who's been cutting with my knife?"

The seventh said: "Who's been drinking out of my cup?"

Then the first dwarf looked round and saw a hollow in his bed. He asked again: "Who's been lying on my bed?"

The others came running up and each one exclaimed as he saw his bed: "Somebody has been lying on mine too."

But when the seventh came to his bed, he saw Snow White lying there fast asleep. He called the others, who ran up and shone their lamps on the bed.

"Goodness gracious! Goodness gracious!" they cried when they saw Snow White lying there. "What a beautiful child!"

They were so enchanted by her beauty that they did not wake her but let her sleep on. The seventh dwarf slept with his companions, one hour in each bed, and in this way he managed to pass the night.

Next morning, when Snow White awoke, she saw the seven dwarfs and felt very frightened, but they were friendly and asked her what she was called.

"I am Snow White," she replied.

"How is it you came to our house?" asked the dwarfs.

She told them how her stepmother had tried to put her to death and how the huntsman had spared her and how she had run the whole day until she had found their house.

Then the dwarfs said to her: "If you will keep house for us, cook, make the beds, do the washing, sewing and knitting, and keep everything neat and clean, you can stay with us and you

shall want for nothing."

"Yes," answered Snow White,
"I will gladly do all you ask."

And so she made her home
with them.

Every morning,
the dwarfs went
into the mountains
to dig for precious
ore and gold, and in the evening
when they returned home their
supper had to be ready. But since,
during the day, the girl was left
quite alone, the good dwarfs warned
her: "Beware of your stepmother.
She will soon find out you are here,
so whatever you do, let no one into
the house."

Now the queen,
after she thought she had eaten
Snow White's lungs and liver, never
doubted that she was once more the
most beautiful woman in the world;
so stepping before her mirror one day
she said:

"Mirror, Mirror, on the wall,
Who is the fairest one of all?"

And the mirror replied:

"Though you, my Queen,
are fair, 'tis true,
Snow White is fairer far than you.

O'er seventh stream and seventh hill,
With seven dwarfs, she's living still."

When the queen heard these words,
her blood boiled with anger, for
the mirror always spoke the truth.
She knew now that the huntsman had
deceived her and that Snow White was
still alive. Day and night she pondered
how she might destroy her, for as
long as she felt she was not the fairest
in the land, jealousy left her no rest.
At last she hit upon a plan. She stained
her face and dressed herself up as
an old pedlar woman. In this disguise,
she set off over the seven hills till she
came to the house of the seven dwarfs.

She knocked at the door, calling: "Fine wares for sale, fine wares for sale!"

Snow White peeped out of the window and called to her: "Good day, good woman, what have you to sell?"

"Good wares, fine wares," she answered. "Laces all of

rainbow hues," and she held one up
that was made of some bright silk.

"Surely I can let the honest woman
in," thought Snow White; so she
unbarred the door and bought the
pretty lace.

"Good gracious, child!" said the
old woman. "What a mess you look!
Come! I'll lace up your bodice
properly for once."

Snow White, suspecting no evil,
stood before her and let the old woman
lace her up so quickly and so tightly
that it took her breath away.

She fell down dead.

"Now you are no longer the fairest,"
said the wicked old woman as she
hastened away.

In the evening, the seven dwarfs came home. You can imagine what a fright they got when they saw their dear Snow White lying on the floor, as still and motionless as a dead person. They lifted her up tenderly and when they saw how tightly laced she was they cut the lace in two.

She began to breathe and little by little came back to life. When the dwarfs heard what had happened, they said: "Why, the old pedlar woman was none other than the queen. In future you must be sure to let no one in, if we are not at home."

As soon as the wicked queen got home, she went straight to her mirror.

"Mirror, Mirror, on the wall,
Who is the fairest one of all?"
And the mirror answered as before:
"Though you, my Queen,
are fair, 'tis true,
Snow White is fairer far than you.
O'er seventh stream and seventh hill,
With seven dwarfs, she's living still."

When the queen heard this, she was so angry that the blood drained from her face, because she saw at once that Snow White must be alive again.

"This time," she said to herself, "I will think of something that will make an end of you once and for all."

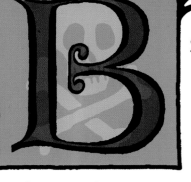

By means of witchcraft, which she understood well, she made a poisoned comb. Then she dressed herself up to look like a different old woman and set out

across the seven hills to the house
of the seven dwarfs. Knocking at
the door, she called out: "Fine wares
for sale!"

Snow White looked out of the window
and said: "Go on your way! I am not
allowed to let anyone in."

"But surely you are not forbidden
to look?" asked the old woman as she
pulled out the poisoned comb and held
it up for her to see.

It pleased the girl so much that
she opened the door.

When they had settled their bargain, the old woman said: "Now just for once, I'll comb your hair properly for you."

Poor Snow White suspected nothing, but as soon as the comb touched her hair, the poison worked and she fell down unconscious.

"Now, my fine lady, you're really finished this time," said the wicked woman, and she made her way home as fast as she could.

Fortunately it was near evening, and the seven dwarfs returned home. When they saw Snow White lying as if dead on the ground, they at once suspected that her wicked stepmother had been at work again; so they searched till they found the poisoned comb.

The moment they pulled it out of her hair, Snow White came to herself again and told them what had happened. Then once more they warned her to be on her guard and to open the door to no one.

As soon as the cruel queen got home, she went straight to her mirror and asked:

"Mirror, Mirror, on the wall,
Who is the fairest one of all?"

And the mirror answered as before:

"Though you, my Queen,
are fair, 'tis true,
Snow White is fairer far than you.
O'er seventh stream and seventh hill,
With seven dwarfs, she's living still."

When she heard these words, the jealous queen trembled and shook with rage.

"Snow White shall die!" she cried. "Yes, even if it costs me my own life."

Then she went to a little secret chamber, which no one knew of but herself, and there she made a poisoned apple. It looked beautiful — white and red cheeked, so that anyone who saw it longed to eat it, but anyone who did so would certainly die on the spot. When the apple was ready, she stained her face, dressed herself up as a peasant woman and set off again to the house of the seven dwarfs. She knocked at the door. Snow White put her head out of the window and called out:

"I must not let anyone in, the seven dwarfs told me not to."

"Quite right," answered the old peasant woman. "But I'll soon have no more apples. Here, I'll give you one."

"No," said Snow White, "I may not take it."

"Are you afraid of being poisoned?" asked the old woman. "See, I will cut this apple in half. I'll eat the white cheek and you can eat the red."

But the apple was so cunningly made that only the red cheek was poisoned. Snow White longed to eat the tempting fruit and, when she saw that the peasant woman was eating it herself, she could resist no longer.

Stretching out her hand, she took the poisoned half, but hardly had the first bite passed her lips than she fell down dead on the ground. The eyes of the cruel queen sparkled with pleasure, and laughing aloud she cried: "As white as snow, as red as blood and as black as ebony! This time, the dwarfs won't be able to bring you back to life."

When she got home, the queen asked the mirror:

"Mirror, Mirror, on the wall,
Who is the fairest one of all?"

At last it replied:

"You, my Lady Queen,
are the fairest one of all."

Then her jealous heart was at rest — at least, as much at rest as a jealous heart can ever be.

When the dwarfs came home in the evening, they found Snow White lying on the ground, and she neither breathed nor stirred. They lifted her up and looked everywhere to see if they could find anything poisonous. They unlaced her bodice, combed her hair, washed her with water and wine, but all in vain; the child was dead and remained dead.

They placed her on a bier and all the seven dwarfs sat round it, weeping and sobbing for three whole days.

At last they made up their minds to bury her, but she looked so like a living being and her cheeks were still so red, that they said: "We can't hide her away in the black ground."

So they made a coffin of transparent glass and laid her in it. In golden letters on the lid they wrote her name and that she was a royal princess. Then they put the coffin on top of a mountain and one of the dwarfs always remained beside it and kept watch over it. Even the birds of the air came and mourned for Snow White;

first an owl, then a raven and last
of all a little dove.

Snow White lay a long time in
the coffin and she always looked the
same, just as if she were fast asleep.
Her skin was still as white as snow,
her lips and cheeks as red as blood,
and her hair as black as ebony.

Now it happened one day that
a prince was in the forest and stopped
at the dwarfs' house. He saw the

coffin on the mountain with the beautiful Snow White inside and, when he had read the golden letters, he said to the dwarfs:

"Let me have the coffin. I'll pay you whatever you like for it."

But the dwarfs said: "Not for all the gold in the world would we part with it."

"Well, then," he replied, "let me have it as a gift, because I can't live without seeing Snow White. I will cherish and love it as my dearest possession."

He spoke so sadly that the good dwarfs had pity on him. They gave him the coffin, and the prince told his servants to bear it away on their shoulders.

Now it happened that they stumbled over a tree stump and jolted the coffin so violently that the poisoned bit of apple Snow White had swallowed fell out of her throat. Before long she opened her eyes, lifted the lid of the coffin and sat up alive and well.

"Where am I?" she cried.

The prince answered joyfully: "You are with me," and he told her all that had happened. He also told her he loved her better than anyone in the whole wide world, and asked her to go with him to his father's palace and be his wife.

Snow White consented and went with him, and the marriage was celebrated with great pomp and ceremony.

Now Snow White's wicked
stepmother was one of the guests
invited to the wedding feast.
When she had dressed herself
very beautifully for the occasion,
she went to the mirror, and said:
"Mirror, Mirror, on the wall,
Who is the fairest one of all?"

And the mirror answered:
"You, my Queen, are fair, 'tis true,
But Snow White is
fairer far than you."

When the wicked woman heard
these words, she was beside herself
with rage and mortification.

At first, she didn't want to go
to the wedding at all, but at the same
time she was so consumed with
jealousy, she felt she would never
be happy till she had seen the young
queen. And so she went to the feast.

As she entered, Snow White
recognized her and nearly fainted
with fear, but red-hot iron shoes had
been prepared for the wicked queen
and she was made to put them on and
dance till she dropped down dead.

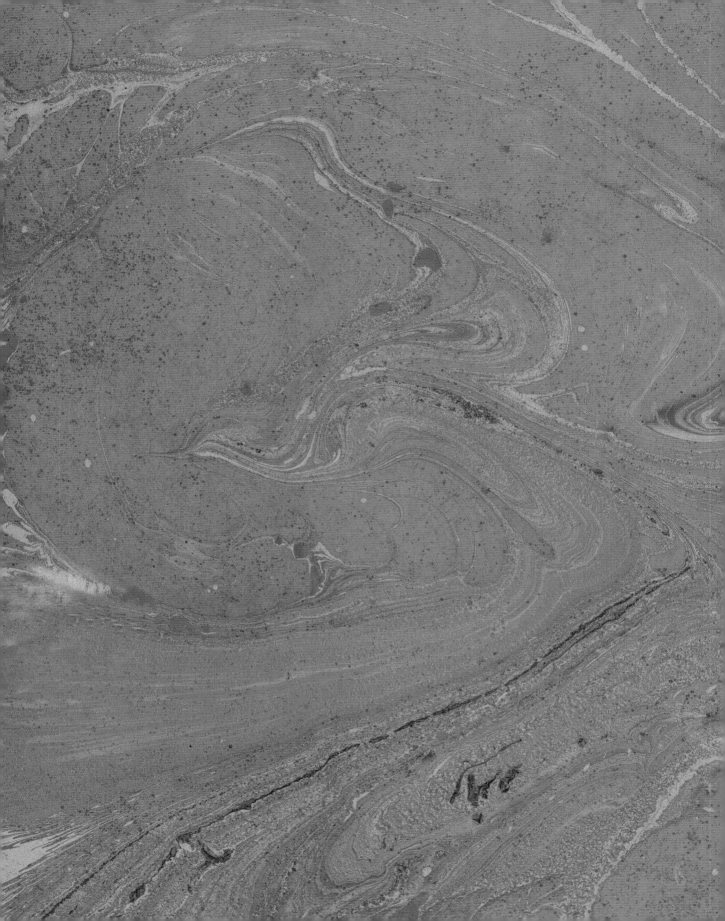

Hansel and Gretel

Told by

THE BROTHERS GRIMM

nce upon a time,
on the outskirts of
a large wood there
lived a poor woodcutter,
his two children and their stepmother.
The boy was called Hansel and the
girl Gretel. The woodcutter had always
little enough to live on, and once, when
there was a great famine in the land,
he could not even provide his family
with their daily bread.

That night, as he was tossing about

in bed, he sighed and said to his wife: "What's to become of us? How are we to support our poor children, now that we have nothing more for ourselves?"

"I'll tell you what, Husband," answered the woman, "early tomorrow morning we'll take the children out into the thickest part of the wood; there we shall light a fire for them and give them each a piece of bread; then we'll go on to our work and leave them alone. They won't be able to find their way home, and we shall thus be rid of them."

"No, Wife," said her husband, "that I won't do. How could I find it in my heart to leave my children alone in the wood? The wild beasts would soon

come and tear them to pieces."

"Oh, you fool!" she said. "Then we shall all four die of hunger, and you may just as well go and plane the boards for our coffins!" And she left him no peace until he gave in.

"But I can't help feeling sorry for the poor children," said the husband.

The children too had not been able to sleep for hunger, and had heard what their stepmother had said. Gretel wept bitterly and said to Hansel: "What will become of us, Hansel?"

"Don't be afraid, Gretel," her brother replied, "I'll find a way of escape." And when their parents had fallen asleep, he got up, slipped on his coat, opened the back door and stole out.

The moon was shining clearly, and the white pebbles which lay in front of the house glittered like pieces of silver. Hansel bent down and filled his pockets with as many of them as he could cram in. Then he went back and said to Gretel: "Be comforted, dear sister, and go to sleep: God will not desert us." And he lay down in bed again.

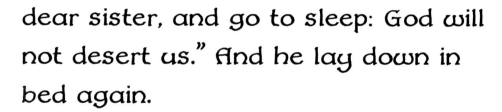

At daybreak, before the sun was up, the woman came and woke the two children: "Get up, you lazybones, we're all going to the forest to chop wood." She gave them each a bit of bread, saying: "Here's something for your dinner, but don't eat it now, for it's all you'll get."

Gretel put the bread in her apron, for Hansel's pockets were already full of pebbles. Then they all set out together into the wood. After they had walked a little way, Hansel stopped and looked back towards the house. This he did again and again until his father noticed and asked him: "What are you peeping at, Hansel? And why are you lagging behind? Just watch where you're going, or you'll trip."

"Oh, Father," said Hansel, "I am looking back at my white cat, which is sitting on the roof, waving goodbye to me."

"You donkey," said his stepmother, "that's the morning sun shining on the chimney." But Hansel had not looked back at his cat; he had been dropping the white pebbles from his pocket on to the path.

When they had reached the middle of the wood, the father said: "Now, children, go and fetch wood, and I'll light a fire so that you won't feel cold."

Hansel and Gretel heaped up a great mountain of brushwood, their father set fire to it and the flames leapt high in the air.

"Now, children," said their stepmother, "lie down by the fire and rest; we are going to chop wood. When we're finished we'll come back and fetch you."

Hansel and Gretel sat down beside the fire, and at midday ate their little bits of bread. They heard the strokes of the axe, so they thought their father was quite near.

But it was not an
axe that they heard,
only a bough he
had tied to a dead
tree, that was being
blown about by
the wind. And when
they had sat for
a long time, their
eyes closed with
weariness and they
fell fast asleep.

hen they awoke at last it was pitch-dark. Gretel began to cry, and said: "How will we ever find our way out of this wood?"

But Hansel comforted her. "Wait," he said, "till the moon is up, and then we'll find our way sure enough." And when the full moon had risen he took his sister by the hand and followed the pebbles, which shone like newly minted pieces of silver, and showed them the path. They walked all through the night.

At daybreak, they reached their father's house again. They knocked at the door and when their stepmother opened it she exclaimed: "You naughty children, why ever did you sleep so long in the wood? We thought you were never coming home again."

But their father was glad, for his conscience had reproached him for leaving his children behind by themselves.

ot long afterwards there was again great scarcity in the land, and one night the children heard their stepmother saying to their father: "The larder is bare once again; there's only half a loaf left and when that's gone we're finished. We must get rid of the children. We'll lead them deeper into the wood this time, so that they won't be able to find their way out again. There is no other way of saving ourselves."

The man's heart was heavy and he thought: "Surely we should share our last crust with the children." But his wife would not listen to his arguments and did nothing but scold and reproach him. And because he had given in once he was done for, and was forced to do so again.

But the children were awake, and had heard them speaking.

When his parents were asleep Hansel got up and wanted to go out and pick up pebbles again, as he had done the first time, but the woman had barred the door and Hansel couldn't get out. Nevertheless he comforted his sister and said: "Don't cry, Gretel, and sleep peacefully, for God is sure to help us."

Early in the morning, the stepmother got them up and gave them each their bit of bread. It was even smaller than the time before. On the way to the forest Hansel crumbled it in his pocket, and every few minutes he stood still and dropped a crumb on the ground.

"Hansel, what are you stopping

and looking behind you for?" asked his
father.

"I'm looking back at my dove, who is
nodding goodbye to me, Father,"
answered Hansel.

"Fool!" said the wife. "That isn't your
dove, it's the morning sun glittering on
the chimney."

But Hansel went on dropping
his crumbs on the path as they
walked along.

The woman led the children still

deeper into the forest, further
than they had ever been before.

The father lit a big fire once again,
and the stepmother said to them:
"Just sit there, children, and if you're
tired you can sleep a bit. We're going
into the forest to chop wood, and in the
evening when we're finished we'll come
back and fetch you."

At midday Gretel shared her
bread with Hansel, for he had strewn
his along their path. Then they fell
asleep, but evening came and went and
no one had come back to fetch them.

They didn't wake up
till it was pitch-dark,
but Hansel comforted
his sister, saying:
"Wait, Gretel, till the moon rises,
then we shall see the breadcrumbs
I scattered along the path; they will
show us the way back to the house."

When the moon appeared they
got up but they found no crumbs,
for the thousands of birds that fly
about the woods and fields had eaten
them all up.

"Never mind," said Hansel to Gretel.
"You'll see, we'll still find a way out."

But they did not.

They wandered about the whole night and the next day, from morning till evening, but they could not find a path out of the wood. They were very hungry too, for they had nothing to eat but a few berries they found growing on the bushes. At last they were so tired their legs refused to carry them any longer, so they lay down under a tree and fell fast asleep.

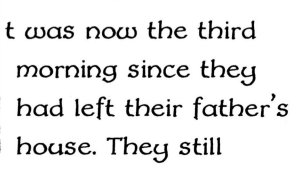

It was now the third morning since they had left their father's house. They still walked on, but only got deeper and deeper into the forest. They knew that if help did not reach them soon, they would die.

At midday they saw a beautiful snow-white bird sitting on a branch, which sang so sweetly that they stopped still and listened to it. When its song was finished, it spread its wings and flew on in front of them. They followed and soon came to a cottage.

The bird alighted on the roof. When they got a little nearer, they saw that the cottage was made of bread and roofed with cakes, while the window was made of transparent sugar.

"Why, Gretel," said Hansel, "we can have a fine feast. I'll eat a bit of the roof and you can eat some of the window, which is sure to be tasty!"

Hansel reached up and broke off a piece of the roof to see what it was like, while Gretel went up to the window and began to nibble at it. Just then a shrill voice called out from the room inside:

"Nibble, nibble, little mouse,
Who's that nibbling at my house?"

The children answered:

"'Tis Heaven's own child,
The tempest wild,"

and went on eating, without stopping.

Hansel, who thought the roof tasted
very nice, tore down a large piece,
while Gretel pushed out a whole round
windowpane and sat down to enjoy it
all the better.

Suddenly the door opened, and an old woman leaning on a staff hobbled out. Hansel and Gretel were so terrified  that they dropped what they had in their hands. But the old woman shook her head and said: "Ah, you dear children! What has brought you here? Come in and stay with me, no harm will come to you."

She took them both by the hand and led them into the house. A delicious meal was laid out on the table — sugared pancakes, apples, nuts and milk. In the back room there were two beautiful beds with clean white sheets, where they lay down after their meal and thought they were in Heaven.

The old woman had appeared to be most friendly, but she was really an old witch who had waylaid the children, and had only built the little bread house in order to lure them in. When anyone came into her power, she killed, cooked and ate him, and made a real feast day of it.

Now witches have red eyes, and cannot see far, but, like beasts, they have a keen sense of smell, and know when human beings pass by. When Hansel and Gretel fell into her hands she laughed maliciously, and said jeeringly: "I've got them now; they shan't escape me."

Early in the morning, before the children were awake, she rose up,

and when she saw them both sleeping
so peacefully, with their round rosy
cheeks, she muttered to herself:
"That'll be a juicy morsel."

She seized Hansel with her bony hand
and shoved him roughly into
a small cage and barred the door.
Let him scream as much as he liked;
it would do him no good.

Then she went to Gretel, shook
her till she awoke, and cried: "Get up,
you lazybones, fetch water and cook
something for your brother. When he's
fat I'll eat him up."

Gretel began to cry bitterly, but
it was no use, she had to obey the
wicked witch. So the best food was
cooked for poor Hansel, but Gretel
got nothing but a crab's claw.

Every morning the old woman
hobbled out to the stable and cried:

"Hansel, put out your finger so that
I can feel if you are getting fat."

But Hansel always held out a bone. The old witch, whose eyes were dim, thought it was Hansel's finger and couldn't understand why he was taking so long to fatten up.

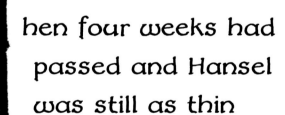

When four weeks had passed and Hansel was still as thin as ever, she lost patience and decided to wait no longer.

"Come here, Gretel," she called out. "Be quick and get some water. Hansel may be fat or thin, I'm going to kill him tomorrow and cook him."

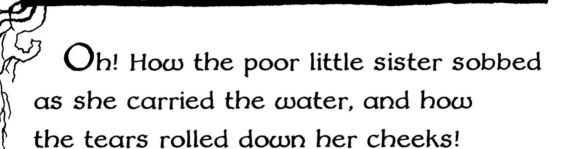

Oh! How the poor little sister sobbed as she carried the water, and how the tears rolled down her cheeks!

"Kind Heaven help us now!" she cried. "If only the wild beasts in the wood had eaten us, then at least we should have died together."

"Just hold your peace," said the old hag. "It won't help you."

Early in the morning Gretel had
to go out and hang the kettle full of
water, and light the fire.

"First we'll bake," said the old woman.
"I've heated the oven already and
kneaded the dough." She pushed Gretel
up close to the oven. The fire was
already burning fiercely and flames
were darting out. "Just creep in, Gretel,"
she said, "to see if it's properly heated,

so that we can shovel in the bread."

Of course, she meant to shut the oven door as soon as Gretel was inside and let the girl bake, so that she could eat her too. But Gretel could see what would happen and said quickly: "I don't know how to do it. How do I get in?"

"You silly goose!" said the hag. "The door is big enough, see, I could get in myself." She crawled towards it and poked her head into the oven. Then Gretel gave her a shove that sent her right in, shut the iron door and drew the bolt.

Gracious! How she howled! It was quite horrible; but Gretel fled, and the wretched old woman was left to perish miserably.

Gretel flew straight to Hansel, opened the cage and cried: "Hansel, we are free! The old witch is dead!"

Hansel sprang out like a bird from a cage when the door is opened.

How they rejoiced, and fell on each other's necks, and jumped for joy and kissed one another.

As there was no longer any cause for fear, they went into the old hag's house, and there they found, in every corner of the room, boxes with pearls and precious stones. "These are even better than pebbles," said Hansel, and crammed his pockets full of them.

"I too will bring something home," said Gretel, and she filled her apron full.

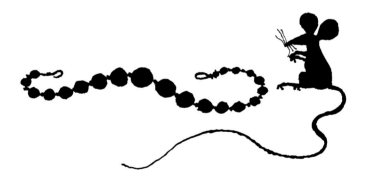

But now," said Hansel, "let's get away from the witch's wood."

When they had wandered about for some hours they came to a big lake.

"We cannot get over," said Hansel.

"But look," answered Gretel, "there's a white duck. If I ask her she'll help us.

"Little white duck!
Little white duck!
Here's two children out of luck.
Please give Hansel and me a ride
To help us reach the other side."

The duck swam up to them. Hansel got on her back and told his sister to sit beside him.

"No," answered Gretel, "that would be too much for the duck. She shall carry us across one at a time."

The good bird did this and soon they were landed on the other side.

As they walked on, the wood gradually became more familiar to them and at length they saw their father's house in the distance. Then they set off at a run, and, bursting into the room, fell into their father's arms.

He had not had one happy hour since he had left his children in the forest; but his wife had died.

Gretel shook out her apron so that the pearls and precious stones rolled about the room, and Hansel threw down one handful after the other out of his pocket.

Thus all their troubles were ended,
and they all lived happily ever after.

And now, my dear,
the tale is over.
Look! there's a mouse
that runs for cover.
Catch him quickly like a cat,
And make yourself
a big fur hat.

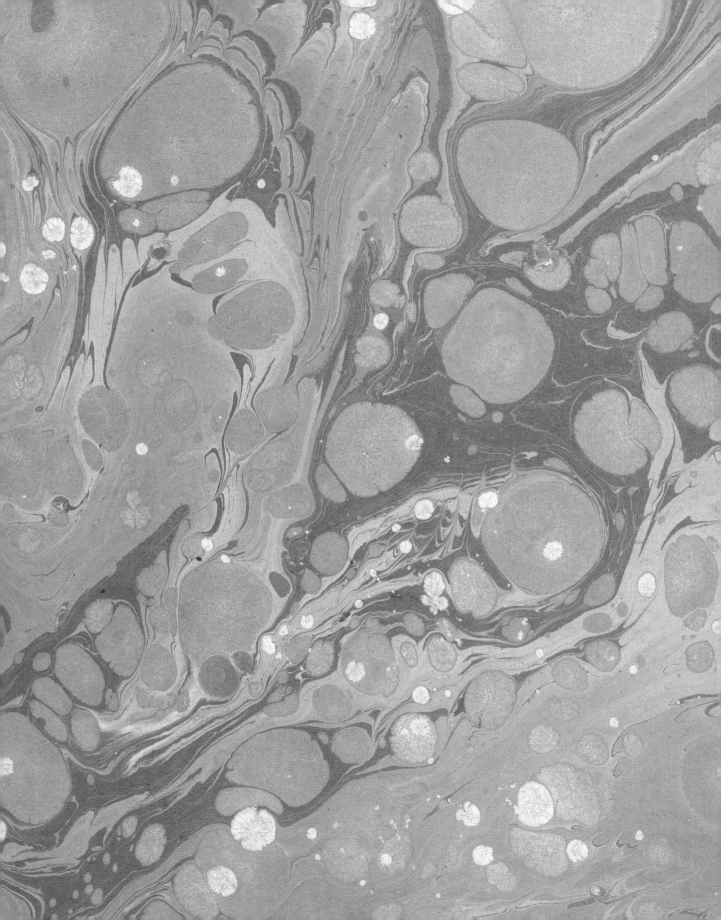

Cinderella

Told by

CHARLES PERRAULT

There was once a gentleman who took, for his second wife, the proudest and most haughty lady that was ever seen. She already had two daughters who were as ill-natured as herself. Indeed, they were like her in all ways.

He, on the other hand, was the father of a young girl whose good and gentle nature was without peer.

No sooner were the wedding ceremonies over, than the stepmother began to show her true nature; she could not endure the virtuous qualities of this pretty girl, who made her own daughters seem all the more odious.

She made her do the meanest tasks
in the house: scour the pots, scrub
the stairs and polish the floors.

The girl had to sleep in a garret
at the top of the house, on a worn-out
straw mattress, while her stepsisters
had rooms with parquet floors,
beds which were the height of fashion
and mirrors so large that they could
gaze at themselves from top to toe.

The poor girl bore everything
patiently, not daring to tell her father,
who would only have scolded her,
for his wife ruled the roost. When the
girl had done her chores, she would sit
down among the cinders and ashes.
For this, she was called Cinder-wench,
although the younger stepsister,

who was not so unkind as the elder sister, called her Cinderella.

In spite of her mean garments, Cinderella was a hundred times prettier than her stepsisters, even though they wore the finest and most fashionable clothes.

I t happened that the king's son was giving a ball to which he invited all the fashionable people. Our young misses were also invited, for they cut quite a dash in society.

Delighted at the invitation,
they busied themselves choosing
the most becoming ball gowns and
head dresses. This made even more
work for Cinderella, for it was she who
had to iron her stepsisters' linen and
pleat the ruffles on their sleeves.

The only talk was about how they should dress.

"For my part," said the elder, "I will wear my red velvet with the English trimmings."

"And I," said the younger, "will wear my gown with the golden flowers.

To crown it all, I shall wear my diamond brooch, which is not exactly an everyday sight."

They sent for the best hairdresser to set their hair in the most fashionable double row of curls, and had their taffeta face patches bought from Madame Faiseuse. They even insisted that Cinderella advise them, for they knew she had good taste. Poor Cinderella gave them the best advice in the world and even offered to do their hair herself, to which they readily agreed. But then they said to her: "Tell us, Cinderella, wouldn't you like to go to the ball?"

"Good ladies," replied Cinderella, "you are making fun of me. Surely this is not a kind thing to do."

"You're quite right," they replied. "How people would laugh if they saw a Cinder-wench at the ball!"

Anyone but Cinderella would have made their hair look wrong, but she made it look as perfect as could be.

For two days, the two young
ladies ate nothing, they were
in such a state of excitement.
They spent the whole time in front
of their mirrors and broke over a dozen
laces trying to look thinner by lacing up
their bodices tighter and tighter.

At last the happy day arrived.

When the two young ladies left
for the ball, Cinderella followed them
with her eyes, so long as she was
able; only when she could see them
no longer did she begin to cry.

Her godmother, who found Cinderella
crying, asked her what the matter was.

"I would like...

I would like..."

But she was crying so much that
she could not finish what she wanted
to say.

Her godmother, who was a fairy,
asked her: "It's the ball you want to
go to, isn't it?"

"Well...yes, it is," sighed Cinderella.

"You're a good girl, I'll see to it that
you go," said her godmother. "Now,

run into the garden, fetch me a
pumpkin and bring it to my room."

Cinderella quickly found
the finest pumpkin in the garden
and brought it to her godmother,
not seeing in the least how this pumpkin
could help her to go to the ball.

Her godmother scooped out all the pulp, leaving nothing but the rind; she struck it with her wand and instantly it was changed into a beautiful golden coach.

Then her godmother peered
into her mousetrap and saw six
live mice; she told Cinderella to lift
the trapdoor just a little. As each
mouse popped out, she tapped it

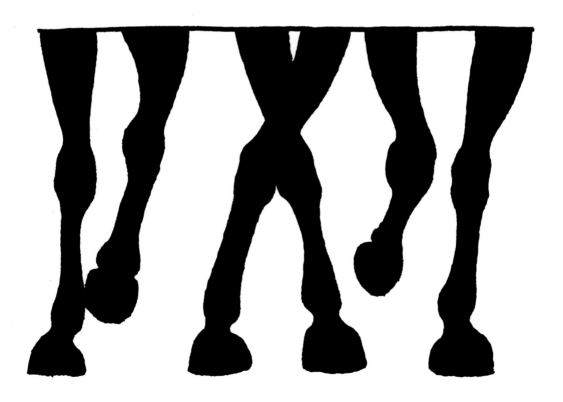

with her wand. In the twinkling
of an eye, each mouse was
changed into a splendid horse,
until there were three matched
pairs of dapple greys.

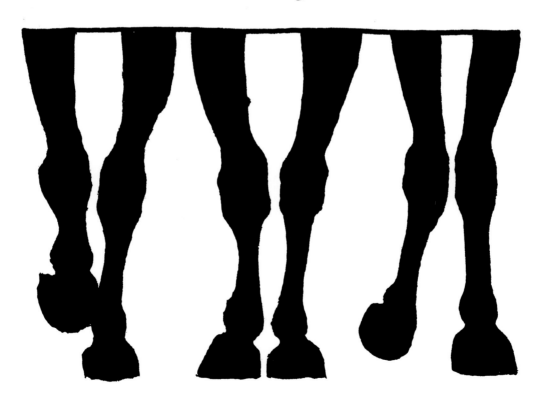

As her godmother was at a loss for something to change into a coachman, Cinderella said she would go and look in the rat trap to see if there was not some rat they could use.

"What a good idea!" said her godmother. "Go and have a look, quickly!"

Cinderella brought the rat trap to her and inside were three big rats. The fairy chose one of the three on account of its fine whiskers. No sooner had

she touched it with her wand,
than it was changed into a
big, fat coachman who had the
smartest moustache anyone
had ever seen.

Then she said: "Go into the
garden, Cinderella, and you will
find six lizards behind the watering
can. Bring them to me!"

No sooner had Cinderella brought
them than they were changed into six
footmen, who jumped up straightaway
behind the coach, all dressed in livery
rich with braiding and frogging, and

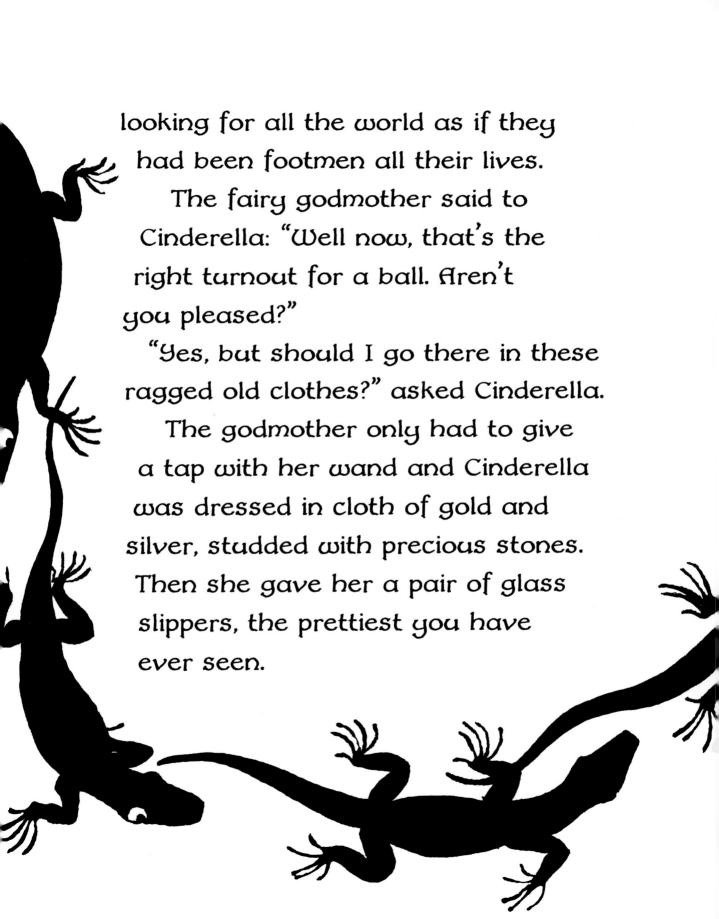

looking for all the world as if they
had been footmen all their lives.

The fairy godmother said to
Cinderella: "Well now, that's the
right turnout for a ball. Aren't
you pleased?"

"Yes, but should I go there in these
ragged old clothes?" asked Cinderella.

The godmother only had to give
a tap with her wand and Cinderella
was dressed in cloth of gold and
silver, studded with precious stones.
Then she gave her a pair of glass
slippers, the prettiest you have
ever seen.

Cinderella climbed
into the carriage
and her godmother
warned her not
to stay beyond midnight, for if she
delayed a moment longer, the coach
would turn back into a pumpkin,
the horses into mice, the footmen
into lizards, and she would find herself
in her old clothes once again.

She promised her godmother that
she would on no account stay at
the ball beyond midnight. And so she
set off, beside herself with pleasure.

The young prince, told that a great princess whom no one knew had just arrived, ran to welcome her. He handed her down from the carriage and then led her to the ballroom where all the guests were gathered.

Silence fell; all eyes were fixed on the beautiful stranger. "How exquisite she is!" said the guests in hushed whispers.

The king himself, old as he was, could not take his eyes off her and said softly to the queen that he had not seen such a pretty and delightful creature for many a year.

All the ladies studied her hairstyle and her clothes so they could copy them the very next day, provided, of course, that they could find such fine materials and a clever enough seamstress.

The young prince seated her at his right hand and then asked her to dance with him. She danced so gracefully that people admired her even more. A most sumptuous feast was served, but the young prince ate not one mouthful, he was so occupied with thinking of her.

During the feast she went to sit next to her sisters, paid them a thousand compliments and pressed on them some of the oranges and lemons that the prince had given her. They were most astonished for they did not recognize her.

While they were talking together, Cinderella suddenly heard the clock strike the last quarter before midnight. She rose immediately, made a deep curtsy to the company and rushed from the room with all speed.

As soon as she reached home, she went to thank her godmother and at the same time to ask her if she could go to the ball again the next night, for the king's son had invited her. Whilst she was telling her godmother about everything that had happened at the ball, the two sisters came banging on the door. Cinderella went to open it for them.

"What a long time you've been," she said, yawning, rubbing her eyes and behaving as if she had just woken up; whereas, of course, there had been no time to sleep since they last parted.

"If you had been at the ball,"
said one of the sisters, "you would not
have been so bored. The most beautiful
princess anyone could imagine paid
us a thousand compliments and
gave us oranges and lemons."

Cinderella did not appear to be
particularly excited by this news;
she did ask them the princess's name,
but they could only say no one knew

who she was. Indeed the prince would gladly pay a king's ransom to know her name.

Cinderella only smiled and said: "Well now, she MUST have been pretty! You look so happy! I wonder if I could see her? Miss Charlotte, could you not lend me your yellow dress, which you wear every day?"

"Really! What an idea!" exclaimed Miss Charlotte. "Lend my clothes to a wretched Cinder-wench? You must think me mad!"

Cinderella was expecting this reply and indeed was quite pleased. She would have been in a fine pickle if her stepsister had agreed to lend her the dress.

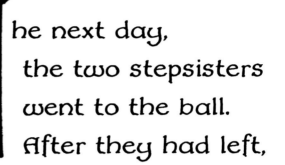

The next day,
the two stepsisters
went to the ball.
After they had left,
Cinderella went too, dressed
even more magnificently than
before. The young prince never
left her side or stopped paying her
compliments. His words, far from being
boring to the young lady, quite put
her godmother's warning from her mind.
Suddenly she heard the first stroke
of midnight when she thought it was
only eleven o'clock. She rose and fled,
nimbly as a deer.

The prince
tried to follow her.
He could not catch her,
but she dropped one of her
glass slippers, and this the prince
picked up and kept.

Cinderella arrived home
quite out of breath — no carriage,
no footmen, wearing her tattered
old clothes.

Of all her finery only a single
glass slipper remained.

At the palace, the guards were
asked if they had seen a princess
leaving the ball.

No! They
had seen only
an ill-dressed wench
who looked more like a peasant
than a young lady.

177

When the two sisters returned, Cinderella asked them if they had enjoyed themselves and if the beautiful young lady had been there again.

"Yes," they replied, "but she fled away as midnight struck, and in such haste that she lost her little glass slipper, the prettiest thing in the world. The prince picked it up and gazed at it for the rest of the ball. He was certainly

very much in love with the owner of
the little glass slipper!"

nd truly it was
so, for only a day
or two later the
young prince had
it proclaimed, with the sound of
trumpets, that he would marry
the girl whose foot fitted the
little glass slipper.

First it was tried on the princesses, then on the duchesses, then on all the ladies of the court, but to no avail. It was brought to the house of the two sisters who did everything they could to squeeze a foot into it,

but again to no avail!

Cinderella, who was looking on and recognized her slipper, said, smiling: "Let me see if it fits me."

Her sisters laughed and made fun of her.

The gentleman who was charged with finding the owner of the little slipper looked carefully at Cinderella.

He saw she was beautiful and agreed to her request, for had he not been ordered to let all the girls try on the slipper?

He made Cinderella sit down and he put the slipper on her foot without the least difficulty. It fitted perfectly.

The two sisters were not a little astonished at this. They were even more amazed when Cinderella pulled the other slipper out of her pocket and put it on as well.

At that moment the fairy godmother appeared and, with a tap of her wand, Cinderella was again dressed more beautifully than all about her. The two sisters saw she was the lovely person they had seen at the ball. They threw themselves at her feet and begged her pardon for all the suffering they had so unkindly caused her.

Cinderella made them rise and told them, while she kissed them both, that she forgave them and asked them to love her for evermore.

Cinderella was escorted to the young prince. He found her more beautiful than ever and, a few days later, they were married.

Cinderella, who was as good
as she was beautiful, found lodgings
for her two stepsisters in the
palace, and on the same day they
were married to two great lords
of the court.